The
Pea
and
the
Princess

To my mum, Ella Grey, and my dad, Peter Grey

THE PEA AND THE PRINCESS
A RED FOX BOOK 978 0 099 43233 3

First published in Great Britain by Jonathan Cape,
an imprint of Random House Children's Books
A Random House Group Company

Jonathan Cape edition published 2003
Red Fox edition published 2004

9 10

Red Fox Books are published by Random House Children's Books,
61–63 Uxbridge Road, London W5 5SA

www.**kids**at**randomhouse**.co.uk
www.**rbooks**.co.uk

Addresses for companies within The Random House Group Limited
can be found at: www.randomhouse.co.uk/offices.htm

THE RANDOM HOUSE GROUP Limited Reg. No. 954009

A CIP catalogue record for this book is available from the British Library.

Printed in Malaysia

Many thanks to KIM for consenting to a guest appearance.

The author and publishers would like to thank The Reader's Digest Assoc. Ltd.
for their permission to reprint an extract from the *Encyclopaedia of Garden Plants and Flowers* © 1997

The Pea and the Princess

MINI GREY

RED FOX

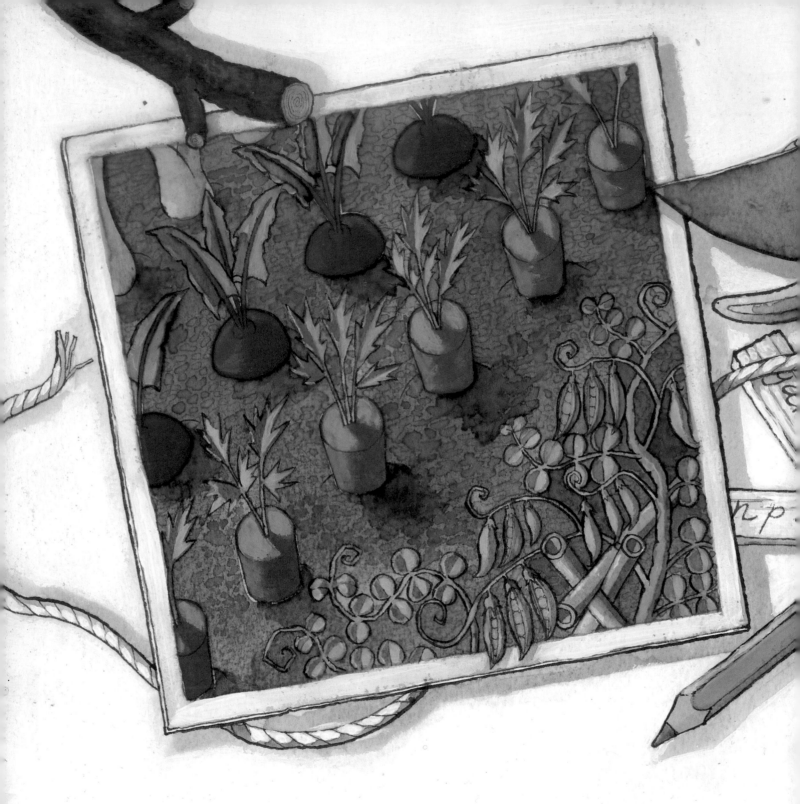

Many years ago, I was born in the Palace Allotment,
among rows of carrot and beetroot and cabbage.

I nestled snugly in a velvety pod with my brothers and sisters.
I felt a tingle. I knew that somehow I would be important.

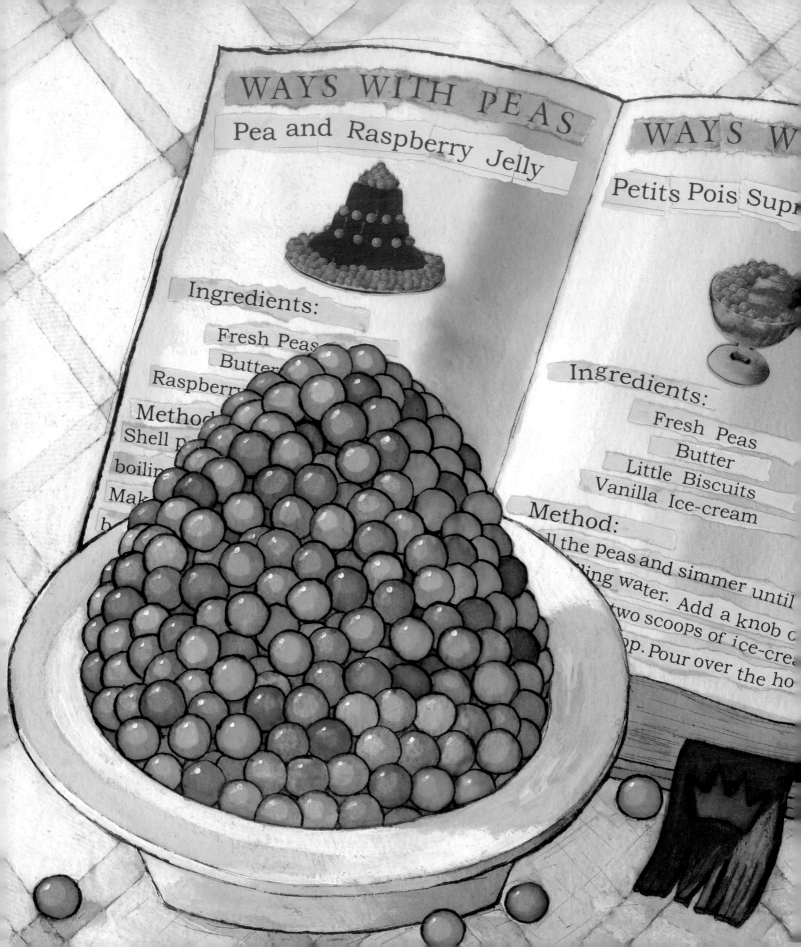

WAYS WITH PEAS
Pea and Raspberry Jelly

Ingredients:

Fresh Peas
Butter
Raspberr

Method
Shell p
boilin
Mak
b

WAYS W
Petits Pois Supr

Ingredients:

Fresh Peas
Butter
Little Biscuits
Vanilla Ice-cream

Method:
ll the peas and simmer until
ling water. Add a knob o
two scoops of ice-crea
p. Pour over the ho

The time came for us to go to the Palace Kitchen.
We were shelled and put in a bowl. We were going
to be part of a New Recipe.
Then, suddenly, I was picked from the pile!
I was put in a little box, with soft tissue to
protect me from bruising.
And I was taken by the Queen.

PEAS

à la Mode

At this point in my story, I'm going to have to give you some background information. Let's start with the Queen.

A year earlier, before I even grew on my pea-plant, the Queen had been nagging her son. "You are nearly thirty-four years old, Prince!" she said. "It really is high time you married. The Public expect it. Your Kingdom demands it. And if you are not married within one year, I shall stop your pocket money."

The Prince got quite a lot of pocket money, and he really didn't want it to be taken away.

"I'll start looking for a bride immediately, Mother," he answered.

And the search began.

The Prince travelled the Known World.
He met princesses of all shapes and sizes,
with a wide range of hobbies and interests.

too grumpy

too sleepy

too pink

too scary

strange pets

None of them seemed really right somehow.

After a year's search, the Prince
returned home, feeling glum.
"RIGHT! THAT'S IT!" shouted
the Queen. She stormed off to the
Palace Kitchen. She came back with
me. In my little box.
"Now," said the Queen,
"listen carefully. This
is something only
Queens know.

"A Real Princess will be able to feel this little pea as she sleeps, even if she is sleeping on top of twenty mattresses and feather beds. And you are going to marry the first girl who can feel this Pea!"

Months passed. I spent most nights in the darkness under a pile of twenty mattresses and feather beds and a princess.

In the morning, each princess would be asked,
"And how did you sleep, my dear?" by the Queen.
The princesses had been properly brought up.
They always answered politely:
"Like a log, thank you, Ma'am" or
"Like a baby, thank you, Ma'am"
and they all said:
"WHAT a comfortable bed!"
They were, as I said, all very polite
princesses.
"The prince will never find his
princess at this rate," I thought
to myself. "I must help.
Somehow."

Onc night, a furious storm raged.
Rain lashed the Palace. Thunderclaps shook the walls.
Lightning flashed through the window panes.
There was a little knock on the Palace door.
A small wet person stood on the doormat.

"Could this be the Real Princess?" gasped the Queen.

Before she could say a word, the small
wet person was put to bed on top
of the twenty mattresses and feather beds.
With me, of course, underneath.
In the darkness under the mattresses,
I recognised the soft snoring.
"I must help," I thought.
I tried jiggling and wriggling.
The snoring carried on quietly.
"I must do something!" I thought desperately.
I inched my way to the edge.
And then I started to climb. Slowly I
struggled to the top of the towering pile.
I softly rolled across the pillow, right to the
girl's ear. "There is something Large
and Round and very Uncomfortable in
the bed under you," I whispered.
And while she slept, I told her about
the Large Round Uncomfortable
thing for three hours.

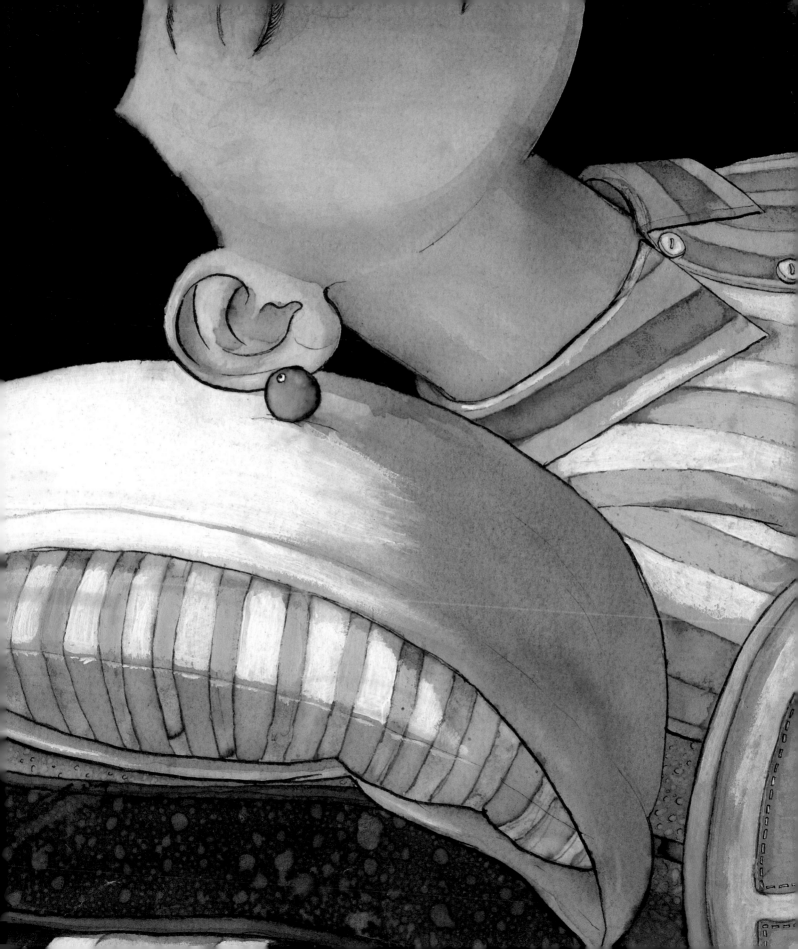

In the morning, the Queen asked
the girl how she had slept.
"Oh, it was awful!" she sighed.
"Something Large and Round and
Uncomfortable was bothering me
all night."

exhibit 235582

The wedding was very grand. The Queen
was interested to meet the new Princess's family.
I'm sure they will all live very happily together.

And as for me? I became a Very Important Artefact.
And now I have my own glass case. I am On Display.
And if you visit the right museum, and look in the right
place, you may chance to see me.

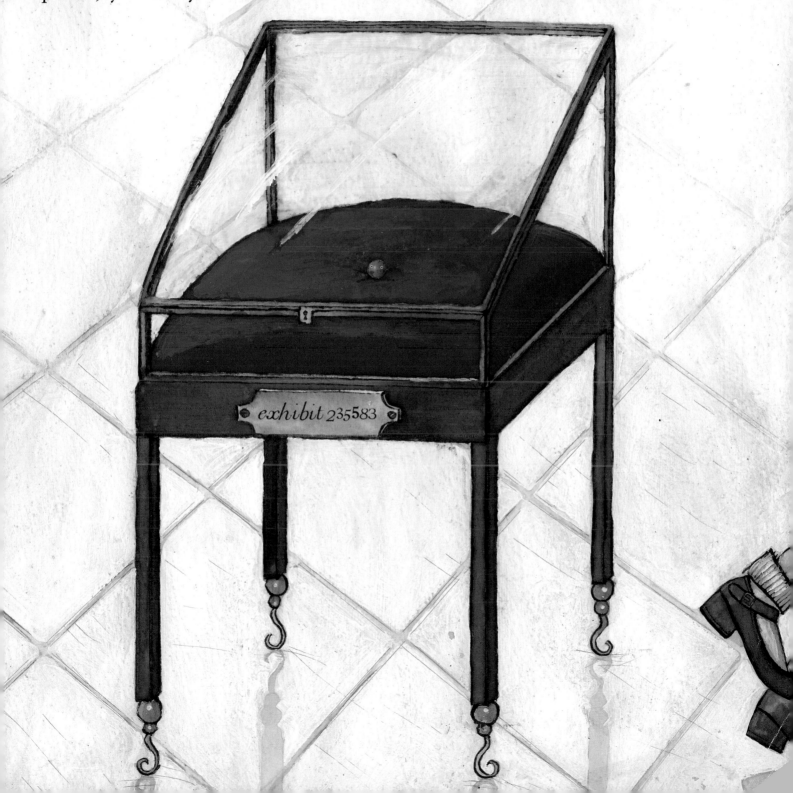

exhibit 235583

More fabulous picture books from

MINI GREY

EGG DROP

BISCUIT BEAR

TRACTION MAN IS HERE

TRACTION MAN MEETS
TURBODOG

THE ADVENTURES OF THE
DISH AND THE SPOON